Fate Amore

Flairs and Glairs
Publication House

"Fate Amore"

ISBN No: " 978-93-91302-29-0"
1st Edition
Language – English and Hindi

Flairs and Glairs
Publication House
Regd. Under MSME Act.

Disclaimer

This is a work of fiction and solely represent the thoughts of the corresponding authors of the articles. Our editors have tried their best to edit the content of all the authors and check the plagiarism.

All the write-ups in this book are unique and are only published in this book.

In case any plagiarism or error is found, only the author is responsible alone, and not the publisher or the Compilers.

Cover Designing and Book Formatting
Shubham Shah and Ishani Agarwal

Acknowledgement

I would like to express my special thanks of gratitude to all my co-authors and team members who helped me to publish this Anthology. Without your hard work, love and support, it would not be possible to publish the book.

We are thankful to Flairs and Glairs Publication, without whom, this project would never have been possible. Moreover a special thanks to our beloved parents, relatives and friends for their continuous support and encouragement towards us in completing this book.

Once again Thanks to all my Co-authors for being a part of this Anthology and also for believing and helping me to publish this Anthology.

Co-Authors

Shubham Shah (Founder Flairs and Glairs)
Ishani Agarwal (Co-Founder Flairs and Glairs)
Aman Sharma (Compiler)
Shree Ram Panday (Co-Compiler)

1. Hrithik Roushan
2. Shalini Soumya
3. Bhavana Manani
4. Aditya Raj
5. Sakshi Mittal
6. Sp Smruti Ranjan Pati
7. Dr. Inderjeet Sharma
8. Shashiinderjeet
9. Shivi Agrawal
10. Bhavika Dudhani
11. Vikash Yadav Vijeta
12. Shalini Kumari
13. Renukuntala Murali
14. Raja Das
15. Aastha Gulati
16. Diksha
17. Kapil Sahare
18. Sabeera Nowreen
19. Barsha Das
20. Dharmesh Sinha
21. Ratnesh Paras Singh
22. Dr. Rakesh Ranjan Mund
23. Megha P. Yadav
24. Er. Mohit A Arya
25. Kameshvar Verma
26. Manisha Singh
27. Vanshika Gupta

28. Vedika Bhoot
29. Babita Goel
30. Saloni Lal Srivastava
31. Mrs. Anmol Kanungo
32. Ankul Mishra
33. Anjaly Sangeeth
34. Deval Tripathi
35. Deenbandhu Chauhan
36. Jaymin Shah
37. Anushka
38. Monica Prajapati
39. Devamrutha S
40. Sourav Malakar
41. Aashtha Sisodiya

Shubham Shah

(Founder- Flairs and Glairs)

Shubham Shah, an entrepreneur at "Flairs & Glairs" a brand with dynamics in events organizing and cultural educational pan INDIA, is a 26yrs old guy who recently has entered the digital platform of imprinting emotions. He has initiated with his own open mic platform to help budding poets and aspiring writers under his brand named as "Teekhe Zasbaaat"

He is a commerce graduate from the Bhagalpur City of Bihar.

He states Writing has impersonated him since childhood and he has now been writing for over a decade!

Cooking, on the other hand, is his passion! He also mentions, trying out new things just tickles him!

When asked sir, Why SPICY EMOTIONS?

He smiled and added, "agar jasbaat teekhe na ho toh wo jasbaat kahan" Spices are all that blends! So do his words!

As a chef, he presents to you his dish! Hot and freshly served! Taste it! Feel it! Enjoy it! You can also find his writing in the Book "Teekhe Zasbaaat" and 50+ Co-authored anthologies. With his passion to explore opportunities across Platforms, he is working with keen devotion and We wish him all the very best for his future ventures.

He is Featured in the International Magazine DeMode for his upcoming solo novel.

He is Approved by Ne8x for its Lit Fest, and is a Golden Star Awards 2020 Winner.

He is a India Book of Records Holder for his Anthology Satrang, and has the Grandmaster title by Asia Book of Records, for the same.

He has also been featured in Prabhat Khabar, Dainik Jagran, and a lot of other Newspapers in Bihar for his achievements.

He has been a proud co-author to

India Book Of Records (Title- Black)

World Book Of Records (Title -15 Wonders of Poetries)

India Book Of Records (Title - Aaina)

Vajra World Records Holder (Title - Gustakhi Maaf Hai)

High Range of Records Holder (Title - Gustakhi Maaf Hai)

Indian Book of Records

(Title - Road from Worst to Best)

Share your reviews on his

INSTAGRAM

@spicy_emotions
@shubham4shah
Or via email on
shubham2shah@gmail.com

To stay tuned to his work and opportunities follow his business Handles

INSTAGRAM   FACEBOOK   YOUTUBE

@flairsandglairs
@teekhezasbaaat

WEBSITE:
https://flairsandglairs.in/
https://flairsandglairs.com/

Ishani Agarwal

(Co-Founder- Flairs and Glairs)

Ishani Agarwal hails from the City of Joy, Kolkata.
She is the co-founder of her Community "Teekhe Zasbaaat" and Flairs and Glairs Publication.
Been a Compiler for 45+ Anthologies, she is in the process for more. Co-authored in 150+ Anthologies. She is a India Book of Records Holder, a Vajra World Records Holder, a High Range of Records Holder, an OMG Book of Records Holder, a Bravo Record holder, a Forever Star Book of World Records and an Indian Book of Records Holder.
Approved by Ne8x for its Lit Fest 2020, and Literary Icon 2020. Also a Golden Star Awards Winner 2020.
She has also been awarded with India Star Republic Award 2021, a part of She Awards by Awards Arc and Winner of Nari Samman 2021 by Literoma.

She is also selected as Best Achiever of the Year by AwardsArc and Most Challenging Compiler Award by Spectrum Awards.
She got her first solo Published,a solo Compilation consisting of first 750 contents of hers, titled "Hand That Burnt While Healing".

She has been featured by the National Magazine "Taree Zameen Par" with the title 'unstoppable'.
Also featured in the International Magazine DeMode for her upcoming solo novel, she is proud to write on social issues, and is happy with the love she is receiving.
Connect with her on Instagram: @Ishani_agarwal_quotes / @compilations_so_far

Aman Sharma
(Compiler)

Aman Sharma is currently **pursuing his Bachelor's in Maths Honours** but he is most interested in expressing his thoughts through his writings. Having a very intellectual mind which has a deep desire to explore the truth and causes of life and its dilemma.

He has already compiled **3** books- **"Wo MAA hi to hai"**, **"DAD: Father, friend and hero"** and **"Love yourself: Finding your Self-worth"** and again he is also a co-author in about **20+ anthologies**.

IG*:* **@aman_shaan**

YourQuote:
https://www.yourquote.in/aman_gaurav

Mystic moon

She shines with mystic beauty bright
Casting silver through the night
Queen of the heavens,
Goddess of light
She is a sweet delight.

Loneliness never hills my heart
When moonlight fills the sky
She is my friend
She is my fate
She is immortal and immaculate.

Her skin is pale and lily-soft
Her hair is dark as night
Her eyes, the stars
Her feet, the earth
And all is clothed in while.

Who knows who the moon is?
Riding through the sky?
Some long forgotten magic
That will not pass us by.

(2)

I do not hide from you the amount of pity mixed with love toward you.

What can a person like me give you? Mostly all the things that one does not want to know.

I tell you about death and life about the mockery of fate and mockery of aspirations, I tell you about what memories of dry days in the head may do and how the desert is colored in the autumn and how laughter is crying of another kind, I teach you with my trembling hand how do you hold life with taste, and how you die in femininity like a fragrant flower that deliberately Refraction at the height of its beauty.

Look at me.

I am not an interesting person, I may be a question that you cannot answer, and this does not prevent me from being clear with you, and for this I tell you that I do not have a beautiful face or a modern car. Tug of her strings, I do not have any talent, I am a bad player, but this does not prevent me from being a sad man, I do not have reassurance, as you see that I am a person afraid of being present, once I tried to be something in this world full of things but I failed, I failed Everything, and here I justify my failure in your love, in this very heavy moment I confess to you that I am a man who is good at chattering about you, who is good at writing poetry Trivial I do not pretend to be a poet or writer. Poets and writers are things, and I failed to be something. In the end I was always waiting for you as a sad child waiting for his lost mother in the crowd.

Thoughts

The clouds that wander through the sky have no roots and no home. And the same is true for your thoughts, and the same is true for your inner sky. Your thoughts have no roots; they have no home; just like clouds they wander. So you need not fight them, you need not be against them; you need not even try to stop thought.

And once you can see that thoughts are floating- you are not the thoughts but the space in which thoughts are floating you have understood the phenomenon of your consciousness. Then discrimination stops: then nothing is good, nothing is bad; then all desire simply disappears, because if there is nothing good, nothing bad, there is nothing to be desired, nothing to be avoided.

You accept, you become loose and natural. You simply start floating with existence, not going anywhere, because there is no goal; not moving to any target, because there is no target. Then you start enjoying every moment, whatsoever it brings- whatsoever, remember. And you can enjoy it, because now you have no desires and no expectations. And you don't ask for anything, so whatsoever is given you feel grateful. Just sitting and breathing is so beautiful, just being here is so wonderful that every moment of life becomes a magical thing, a miracle in itself.

And then, then you know that IN SPACE SHAPES AND COLORS FORM. Clouds take many types of shapes: you can see elephants and lions, and whatsoever you like. In space forms, colors, come and go. But neither by black nor white is space tinged. But whatsoever happens, the sky remains untouched, untinged. In the morning it is like a fire, a red fire coming from the sun, the whole sky becomes red; but in the night where has that redness gone? The whole sky is dark, black. In the morning, where has that blackness gone? The sky remains untinged, untouched.

And this is in fact the case. When you think you are tinged, it is just thinking. When you think that you have become good or bad, sinner or sage, it is just thinking, because your inner sky never becomes anything- it is a BEING, it never becomes anything. All becoming is just getting identified with some form and name, some color, some form arising in the space- all becoming. You are a being, you are already that- no need to become anything.

Look at the sky: spring comes and the whole atmosphere is filling birds singing, and the flowers and the fragrance. And then comes the fall, and then comes summer. Then comes the rain- and everything goes on changing, changing, changing. And it all happens in the sky, but nothing tinges it. It remains deeply distant; everywhere present, and distant; nearest to everything and farthest away.

Shree Ram Panday
(Co-compiler)

श्री राम पाण्डेय एक विद्यार्थी होने के साथ एक सुलझे व्यक्ति भी है। जितनी ताकत इनके मुस्कान में है, उतनी ही इनके कलम से पिरोएं शब्दो में झलकता है। आप सोच रहे होंगे वो कैसे, तो यूँ समझ लीजिए की दोनों कातिलाना है। हँस के भी आप के दिल को घायल कर सकते और अपने शब्दों से भी।

विधाता

ज़िन्दगी देने वाला विधाता बैठा है कही
खबर है उसको सब फिर भी रूठ बैठा है कही
ज़िन्दगी मुश्किल तो नहीं
पर आसान भी नहीं दिया उसने
कर्म के राह पर भाग्य बनाता है वो
किस्मतों का लकीर सजाता है वो
वजूद है, उस विधाता की इस दुनिया में कही
यूँ ही नहीं ज़िन्दगी देकर मिटाता है वो....!!!

Hrithik Roushan

हितिक रौशन एक अच्छे स्टूडेंट होने के साथ एक **दिलचपस** और **हँसमुख व्यक्ति** भी है, ये अपने काम के प्रति जागरूक होते है साथ ही किसी भी चीज को बड़े प्यार से समझने की क़ाबिलियत रखते है , इनको लिखने का शौख बचपन से ही है,

इनको शायरी लिखना काफी अच्छा लगता है जितने रोमांटिक इनकी शायरी होती है उस से ज्यादा ये है।

भाग्य विधाता

क्या खेल है तेरा हे भाग्य विधाता
तू दुनिया के है कई रंग दिखाता
कहीं भेद से भरा ये दुनिया
कहीं गंगा सी निर्मल है
कहीं कपटी कई रूपो वाला
कहीं पवन सा चंचल है
कहीं है वैहशी रावण जैसा
कहीं राम सा कौशल है
कहीं है राजा कहीं है रंक
कहीं है ज्ञानी कहीं उदंड
कहीं है पूरे मन से स्वस्थ
कहीं है मानव पूरा अपंग
कहीं है हिर्दय कोमल जैसा
कहीं है मानव दुर्योधन जैसा
अजीबो गरीब दुनिया के दाता
क्या खेल है तेरा हे भाग्य विधाता
तू दुनिया के है कई रंग दिखाता

Shalini Soumya

Shalini Soumya **(Tannu)** is a student of **Class 12ᵗʰ (Science)** and writing for her is like a refreshing cup of coffee and it makes her feel lively. Pouring her heart out onto the paper makes her feel light.

She has contributed her writings in **3 anthologies- "Wo MAA hi to hai", DAD: Father, friend and hero"** and **LOVE YOURSELF: Finding your self-worth".**
IG: @soumya_shalini

Thoughts

Thoughts exist separate from you, they are not one with your nature, and they come and go- you remain, you persist. You are like the sky: never comes, never goes, it is always there. Clouds come and go, they are momentary phenomena, and they are not eternal. Even if you try to cling to a thought, you cannot retain it for long; it has to go, it has its own birth and death. Thoughts are not yours, they don't belong to you. They come as visitors, guests, but they are not the host.

Watch deeply, then you will become the host and thoughts will be the guests. And as guests they are beautiful, but if you forget completely that you are the host and they become the hosts, then you are in a mess. This is what hell is. You are the master of the house, the house belongs to you, and guests have become the masters. Receive them, take care of them, but don't get identified with them; otherwise, they will become the masters.

The mind becomes the problem because you have taken thoughts so deeply inside you that you have forgotten completely the distance; that they are visitors, they come and go. Always remember that which abides: that is your nature. Always be attentive to that which never comes and never goes, just like the sky. Change the gestalt: don't be focused on the visitors; remain rooted in the host; the visitors will come and go.

Of course, there are bad visitors and good visitors, but you need not be worried about them. A good host treats all the guests in the same way, without making any distinctions. A good host is just a good host: a bad thought comes and he treats the bad thought also in the same way as he treats a good thought. It is not his concern that the thought is good or bad.

Because once you make the distinction that this thought is good and that thought is bad, what are you doing? You are bringing the good thought nearer to yourself and pushing the bad thought further away. Sooner or later, with the good thought you will get identified; the good thought will become the host. And any thought when it becomes the host creates misery- because this is not the truth. The thought is a pretender and you get identified with it. Identification is the disease.

Only one thing is needed: not to be identified with that which comes and goes. The morning comes, the noon comes, the evening comes, and they go; the night comes and again the morning. You abide: not as you, because that too is a thought- as pure consciousness; not your name, because that too is a thought; not your form, because that too is a thought; not your body, because one day you will realize that too is a. Just pure consciousness, with no name, no form; just the purity, just the formlessness and namelessness, just the very phenomenon of being aware- only that abides.

If you get identified, you become the mind. If you get identified, you become the body.

Bhavana Manani

Bhavana Manani, is a senior student at a college affiliated to **Osmania University, Hyderabad,** pursuing Bachelors of Commerce.

A commerce student by profession and a writer by passion. She believes in "either do something that is worth writing or write something that is worth reading." "Writing is a FEELING only a few can feel!" is what she says.

She is a published author of the book **"Mystery Revealed – Turns & Twists of Life."** She also contributed to various anthologies as a co-author. Some of them are **"Wo MAA hi to hai", "Dad - father, hero and friend."** Her dedication is what sets her apart from anybody else.

For more of her writings, visit;

Your quote: https://www.yourquote.in/manani

God's Untold Plan!!

Ever believed in fate?
Meeting someone unexpectedly may be fate!
But then, understanding each other,
Completing the journey from
Being a stranger to close friends
Is where your efforts and time matters!

Yes,
I met her as a stranger
We fought on a silly thing at that moment.
But trust me,
It was the first time
I felt bad after a silly fight with a stranger
After all she was nothing to me then!
But yet seemed to have a connection!!

Yes! May be because it was God's untold plan!
Now?
It's been 10 years
We are damn good friends...

Yes!
I do believe in god's magic.
But this time I have experienced it!

Though different colleges, different streams,
Still we manage to give time to each other
Understand and guide each other on various matters just like
soul mates!

Should I reveal the name of the person?
She is Soundarya, my closest buddy!

Describing her could leave a writer like me with no words. Because when everyone else was busy in some or the other work, we were unknowingly busy creating memories then! Realising the importance of it today!

Heartfully thank you **Soundarya** for being by my side in this rollercoaster life &, also for being a part of a decade of my life. And this is a small write-up from this writer on this occasion, because I believe in the power of words.

Just wanted to tell the world out
That yes! Good people like you do exist.
Trust God, have patience!
Because he is the real writer of every individual's FATE
AMORE!

Aditya Raj

Aditya Raj is presently a student of grade **Twelfth.** He has a prolific intrest towards quotes and short poem writing. He began his journey of writing at the age of **13 years**.

माँ

साँसों की मेरे जीवन डोर हो तुम
जिस किनार से बहुँ वो छोर तुम
मेरे जीवन की राह तुमसे है
मेरी अंधेरी रातो की सवेर हो तुम

है यादें बचपन की अब तक ज़ेहन में
रूठना मेरा और मनाना तेरा मुझे
कभी देखा नही गुस्सा मैंने आँखों मे
कितना प्यार दिया है तूने मुझे

उफ़्फ़ ना कहे सहकर सब कुछ
कैसे सब कर लेती हो
कभी चंडिका कभी चाँद सी
सब रूप में बस जाती हो

लक्ष्य मेरे जीवन का उद्देश्य तुम हो माँ
तुम बिन जीवन मेरा जैसे कुछ नही है माँ

Sakshi Mittal

Sakshi Mittal is a student who started writing in this lockdown to express her feelings. She loves to read and wanted to help poor people in her entire life. She is from Vrindavan, U.P (Uttar Pradesh). She is **12th Class** student with **PCM** scheme. In a short interval of time she has written books. If you want to read her writeups more, then you can follow her on insta **@writting_panda**

Betiyaan

Osh ki ek bund hoti hai betiyaan
Sparsh khurdura karke ro deti hai betiyaan
Roshan karega beta ek hi kul ko
Do-do kul ko roshan kar deti hai betiyaan
Koi nahi hai yha ek dusre se kam
Agar beta heera hai to moti hai betiyaan
Kaato ki rah par khud chalti rahengi
Oro ke lie fuul bichati rahengi
Vidhi kaa vidhan yahi hai samaj ki paramparah
Apne priyo ko chod apne piya ki ghar chal deti hai betiyaan
Hota hai ajeeb sa maahol jab chod ke chali jaati hai yeah
Sirf ghar kaa hissa nahi
Maa-baap ke dil kaa tukda hoti hai betiyaan
Kitna rula jaati hai betiyaan
Yeah to unhi se pucho jinke paas hoti hai bitiyaan
Yeah main nahi kehti
Yeah to khuda kehta hai
Jab vo kisi se kush hota hai to use deta hai betiyaan.
Jesi bhi hai betiyaan hoti hai pure ghar kaa tudka

Meri maa

Maa meri pyaari pyaari
Maa meri nyaari nyaari

Roj gussa karti hai
Phone cheen kar rakh leti hai
Esi tarike se voh hume sulati hai
Ja vo uthti hai to paani daal kar uthati hai
(Jesa bhi hai uska yeah tarika bhut pyaara lagta hai)

Deti saari cheeze hai maa
Din bhar kitchen mein lagi rehti maa
Sone se phele roj puchti
Bta do kya khana hai kal
Bhuka nahi dekh sakti vo kisi ko
Chae hum ho yaa papa
Apne lie banane mein aalas aata hai use
Or hamare lie kud-kud kar banati hai maa

Devi jesi maa hai meri
Saare jag mein nyaari maa hai meri
Enke gusse ki to aadat padh gai hai
Bin uske neend naa aati
Bin uske neend naa khulti

Papa ke aane par bachi ban jaati hai
Or jab mishmisi aati hai to humse bhi choti ban jaati hai

Jesi bhi hai maa meri bachi hai
Jesi bhi hai maa meri bachi hai

SP Smruti Ranjan Pati

SP. Smruti Ranjan Pati, a boy from a small town Jagatsinghpur with big dreams and believes in the power of pen!

'Believing yourself & your dreams can make you what you think' & he strongly believes in this pure imagination.

According to him, **writing is a way to express the thoughts of love, science & experiences.** He started writing from the time when he didn't know what he was writing, either it was correct or not!

It became a part and parcel of his fast racing life!

<u>साल २००२</u>

एक छोटे से हॉस्पिटल में एक छोटे से बच्चे का जन्म,
ना थी उसे कोई भी चीज की खुशी ना थी उसे कोई भी चीज का गम,
साल बढ़ते गई मुस्कान बढ़ता गया धीरे धीरे बेटा स्कुल चलता गया,
एकदम मस्ती मी कट रहा था उसका जीवन खेल कूद पढ़ाई दोस्ती में था बस उसका मन,
दोस्तो के साथ कुछ भी करने का काम सुभा शाम डाट होती नहीं थी कम,
कुमार सानू की आवाज में (कुछ ना कहो) में थम गया उसका मन,
अब क्या करे प्यार चीज ही ऐसा है जो बंद कर्देता है दिल की धड़कन,
फिर..फिर क्या आंखे मिली प्यार हुआ इकरार हुआ बस हर दिन एक नया त्योहार हुआ,
धीरे धीरे ठीक ठाक जीवन में तूफान की आने की खामोशी कुमार सानू की आवाज में (आंखे है भारी भारी) की मधोसी,
सब एकदम थम सा गया समय का पहिया रुक सा गया,
सब बिगड़ गया खिलता हुआ जीवन एक अंधेरी राह में मूड गया,
बच्चा क्या भी करे !
है तो इंसान ही !!
और था जीवन में कुछ करने की चाह भी !!!
हां याद अती थी वो पर एकदिन एहसास हुआ
ये तो जीबन का सुरूबात हुआ,
समय एक नई मुस्कान के साथ निकल गया ।
जीवन एक नेइए रहा में मूड गया ।
जीवन का पहिया आगे बढ़ता गया
बहुत दिन के बाद समझ आया ये सब है मोह माया,
जब अंधेरी में साथ छोड़ देता है अपना साया,

अरे ये तो जीवन का उसूल है जो भी आया जिंदगी में कुछ ना कुछ ज्ञान देके चला गया ।

उस वक्त समय कुछ अलग था

और एक बात बताऊं साल २००२ का बच्चा कोई और नहीं में था !

ये थी मेरी 19 साल की कहानी

सपना कुछ अलग था समय कुछ अलग था पर 19 साल ने सिखादीया जिंदगानी ।

पर भूल ना मत यारो

ये है जिंदगानी, हर दिन एक नेई कहानी।

Dr. Inderjeet Sharma

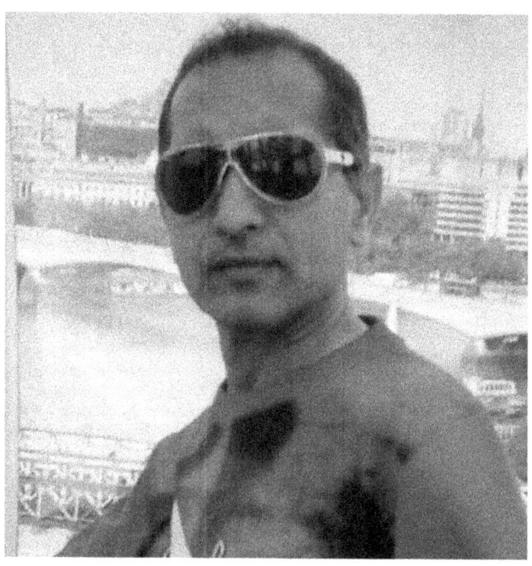

Literature has always contributed as an important medium of inspiration and Direction for the coming generations.

Dr. Inderjeet Sharma is a very simple human being, dedicated and devoted to understanding the depth of art, culture and literature. He finds the rise of the knowledge of the entire world, inspired by the great ancient Vedic knowledge of India.

As a published writer, he has contributed as a co-author in more than **40 Anthologies**.

If his writing is to be summed-up in one line, it will be
"The pen filled with the ink of energy and inspiration"

Time-Escalator

Destiny is the index of the incidents fixed by the
Creator of the Universe himself for organizing its functioning
in an order
One has to act scene by scene according to the direction of
the Fate
Along with the five basic elements of the life, the element of
realization is also very important to enjoy the life to its fullest
Destiny rules you
Fate decides the movement and calculations of Time
Time is unstoppable
It decides your movement
It decides your fate
It's an escalator of your life
and the control of escalators
is somewhere else
don't let anything else drive your life
Move with the time holding the
master key under your control
Time may be unstoppable but
you can turn its track
You can hold the halter in your hands
You can make it favourable

जिस राह पे यह वक्त तुम्हें ले चले, चलते रहो
बस याद रहे, वक्त की चाबी तुम्हारे हाथ हो

Time impact

Oh God of gods, with your powers only, the World
Sleeps and awakens
Oh God of gods, with your magic, the World
Stimulates its functioning
You are super among supers
Your desire makes the World alive
You set the priorities of the World
You allot the slots of Time favorable or
unfavorable in life's journey
What humans have to learn is ' compatibility with
the Time '
Time is a dominating factor in one's life
The shades of Time turn grey and pink in the journey
incidents change their impact in the rotation
Don't run to catch the Time but follow and
cross its path
Good or Bad, Time will come and go
Never let the small events overshadow your Life
Never let the Time to come between you and your Smile
Life is too short
Life is to experience the known and unknowns
Life is to live...

वक्त का क्या है, आता जाता रहता है सदा
ज़िन्दगी वो ही है जो मुस्कुराते ही सदा गुज़रे

Shashiinderjeet

Veena Sharma (Shashiinderjeet) from Jammu
Published author **'Aviral dhara'**
Co-author in more than **30 anthologies.**
Loves Writing, Painting, and fashion designing

State Best Teacher Awardee Veena Sharma, a lecturer by profession, wrote her first story **'Mera sapna'** when she was only nine years old.
She writes in Hindi, Urdu and English. Writing is her passion, she can never think about herself without writing. Her writing skill is versatile. She believes in **'vasudev kutumbkam'**

A Wish

My wish to love you
From the core of my heart
Will be fulfilled by the blessings
Of Almighty
O my sweetheart
The quest of love is as pure as gold
I feel the positive vibes
Nobody will dare to hold
As true love is welcomed by all
I want to share all my life with you
If you accept my proposal
Want to see you dear as my wife
Made for each other, have to prove honesty
Living together in every sphere of life
It will be our duty
To fulfill each other's wishes in life
Though fate plays great role in life
Yet blessings are precious
To share love in life

Love Is Power

Love is…
The power of exhortation,
Away from frails and fractions,
One feels edification in love.
Eccentric emotions
Being whimsical,
Have no place in love.
Love in heart
Efflorescence the garden,
Makes the heart full of eminence.
Love is above all.

Shivi Agrawal

Shivi Agrawal is **a student of 11th commerce**. Well, she has just started this beautiful and adventurous journey by this 1st book. She is from Vrindavan, U.P (Uttar Pradesh). **Writing is just not a hobby for her; this is what which makes her feel blessed and happy every single time** and she hope that her words can help you to express what you feel too.

INTEZZAR

Humme smjh nahi aya
Orr wo ho gya
Humne bss dekha tha unhe
Orr unka dil kho gya
Pehla pyr tha unka
Orr phir dono ka akhri hogya
Naa naa krte
Humme pyrr unhi se ho gya
Humnedrd diye
Unhone haskr seh liye
Humari haa ke inntezaar m
Unhone hrrr jakhm jee liye
Humne muskya
Toh khud ko humme saup diya
Jis din humne haa kaha
Uss din duniya se nata tod liya
Kehte h wo
Nasha kro toh aisa jiska tod na ho
Isliye humse mohbbat krr baithe wo
Humne haskrr puch liya
Agr mana krdete toh kya krte tum
Unhone ankho m dekhte hue kaha
Humne kaha tha na
Ki mohbbat ke nashe ka koi tod nhi
Humare intezar ki koi seema nahi
jindagi jitni bhi h humari
Apa nahi toh
Apke haseen intejaar ke.
Bharose kategie humari

NATURE

Khawish kuch iss trh h
Ki tumhare sth rehna he
Ek sapne se bada hai

Iss 21st century m
Sirf tumhara deedar bada hai

Jaha milte the tum sirf sukun ki trh
Aja uss sukun ka
Sauda bada hai

Subh ki pheli chai chidiyo ke sth
Aja uska sirf sapna bada hai

Wo sunheri chaou (shadow) ka
Milna abb mushkil se bada hai

Kaha kho gyi wo saf hawa
Jiska milna janglo me basa hai

Aja kisi ka sathi hathi nahi hai
Aja kisi ki baate shero se nahi hai

Bass jo gaye hai hum 4 deewari mai jabse
Tabse sukoon ka sauda bada hai

Bhed bbaad me aise kho gye hum
Ki raaho me milna he mushkil se bada hai

Bhavika Dudhani

Bhavika Dudani, a **19 year** old introvert **writing since 8 years.** She strongly believes that **"Poetry is fusion of emotions penned to express"** She resides in the city of lights and dreams-Mumbai. Decanting her thoughts brings her solace. She puts her emotions into red, blue and black.
You can reach her at:
Mail- bhavikadudani48@gmail.com
Instagram- @bhavi_dudani25

Do Me

Hold me hostage in your arms,
fixed and tight
Give it to me just one more time
Let me put that warmness in my rhyme.

Grab my waist and pull my gown
Lick it all, up and down
I want to be your personal scown.

Coax my thighs, running your fingers high
Press yourself to me
Let me feel something I cannot deny
Moans, thrusts, gasps do it all to me, don't let it dry.

Snatch my arms and grace your lips
All over my body now make it flip
Get your weapon and let it slip
Deeper and harder make all of it trip.

Unhurried and swift, let it all mix
Howling and raging, hold my wrist
Make me not wanting to resist
Tease me, hunt me, and make it explicit.

Don't Let Me Go

You kept rumbling into my mind
Like you were obtuse and blind
Could you let me, let you go?
Don't hold me so tight and leave me so slow
We aren't destined and you know
Still can we have a trivial show?
Maybe we make it to the sun and snow.
Now, why are you letting me go?
I want to stay along, like that birthmark on your toe
I want to stay along, like your car holds that bugatti logo
I want to stay along, like the tattoo on your elbow
I want to stay along, watch you learn watch you grow
I want to stay along, having it all, defeating your foe
So baby, even when I say let me go,
Hold me tight and take me home.
I want to stay along, don't set me loose don't have me
shoved!

Vikash Yadav Vijeta

मेरा नाम विकाश यादव 'विजेता' है। मेरा जन्म **7 अक्टूबर 2004** में उत्तर प्रदेश के गाजीपुर जिले में हुआ था। मैं अभी **12वीं का छात्र** हूं। मुझे लेखन कार्य में रुचि बचपन से ही है। मैं खुद ही नहीं समझ पाता हूं कि यह कला मेरे अंदर कैसे आई। मैं इसे ईश्वर का वरदान समझकर साहित्य साधना में लगा हूं। **साहित्य** और **समाज सेवा** ही मेरी प्राथमिकता है।

करूणामय प्रेम

वह बिलख बिलख कर रोती
करूणा की गीत सुनाती
आंखों में क्या रखा है
जब मन हो भर आतीं

जब मिले थे प्रेम के धागे
सुनहरे स्वप्न जगे थे
हर उपवन खिल उठा था
कुछ फूल नये उगे थे
जब घायल मन की आंहें
इन लहरों से टकरातीं
करूणा की गीत सुनाती

अंतर्मन की ना सुना
फोड़ा सर पटक पटक कर
जीता कितने दिन आखिर
ऐसे ही सिसक सिसक कर
झरनों से गिरता पानी
पत्थरों से जब टकराती
करूणा की गीत सुनाती

है दर्द अनंत तुम्हारे
है व्यथा असीम तुम्हारी
वह भी पागल सा बैठा
वह भी बैठी बेचारी
आंगन में होती बारिश
जब दूर गगन से आतीं
करूणा की गीत सुनाती

एक शख्स रोता जा रहा है

कुहरा आकाश पर छाता रहा है
हमको पागल कहा जाता रहा है

देख हकीम तेरे फैसले कैसे रहे हैं
भर सफर एक शख्स रोता जा रहा है

खूब हम से दुश्मनी किया उसने
अब सुना हूं वह बहुत पछता रहा है

ताकि बदल ना पाए इस शहर के मंजर कभी
वह मेरी आवाज दबाता रहा है

चाह कर भी अदालत कभी न्याय कर नहीं सकती
के हर घटना पर सियासत का पर्दा रहा है

Shalini Kumari

Hey everyone, Shalini here.

I love to write my poems about any special bond and **about the things that are going around** me.

I would like to tell you that I have presented my two beautiful creations hope you'll love it.

Writing something is the best way to express ourselves. Not only that we can portray ourselves through writing.

To be honest, in my opinion writing poems or any story is like creating your own world whereas with the help of your skill you can make peoples aware of bad practices and anything wrong that is going behind ourselves.

You May Have Seen

What's the mistake I have done?
Please tell me someone
So that I can recover it soon
The society let to feel me inferior like in bunch of stars
there's a moon
Which is the thing that I can't do?
Then why separating me I'm asking to you.
The country will develop...
But what's about your mentality..??
It's like a stamp on envelope
Can't be removed
We'll evolve but can your thought be improved?
It's so sad to tell me that thus
You all will take your eyes away
When some injust is done with us.
You'll be not there.
When we are in trouble.
Then we are trying to tell this but "Don't say!"
Don't cover me.
I will take the step first.
Just do your work that is to see.

Cause It's You Who Does Matter

Just take some time for yourself
Sit peacefully to think about yourself
I know it's very difficult to manage this busy day
But can we take a couple of minutes from our today
Trust me you'll feel better
It's only you who does matter
I wondered this feeling when I'm sitting quietly
'Just do whatever you want to!' say it to yourself politely
Trust me you'll feel better
Cause it's only you who does matter.

Renukuntla Murali

Renukuntla Murali, **M.A., M.Phil., M.Sc., Psych., PG Dip.,** in Light Music. **Bilingual Poet** (Telugu & English) **Singer, Writer & Author** working as **Lflhm** at Mpps Gurijakunta, Mandal Cherial, Siddipet, Telangana. He is the **Dist. best teacher awardee.** He is the founder & director of **"Sanath Institute of English"**, Jangaon Estd. in **1989.** He has written **350 poems in English** & received more than **175 awards**, appreciative certificates in the challenges held by different organizations such as **Pen Brew Community team & Nazm-e-hayath team, The WU Writer & Untouched Emotions, Million writers** etc. National & International level. He has written **75 poems in Telugu** & published in **40+ anthologies.**

Success in life

There are no shortcuts
To success in life
Success depends
Upon your hard work,

A person who wants
To success in life
Must work hard and
And dedication,

There are four D's
Determination
Dedication
Devoted work and
Dogged pursuit,

Positive attitude
Persons can achieve
Positive results
Negative attitude
Persons can achieve
Nothing results,

Successful persons
Always must have
Positive attitude
And achieve great
Goals,

Success can enlighten
You throughout the
Life and enrich
Honor forever"

Smile Of Child

The smile of child
Is like a layer of the
Milk
The smile of the child
Is like a jasmine flower
The smile of child is
Like a lily flowers,

The smile of the child
Is so cute and honest
The smile of child is
Like the honey
The smile of child is
Amiable,

The smile of child
Can save the many
Suicides of the parents
Because though the
Parents fight with each
Other and discussion
Takes place only the
The smile of child can
Make them to love and
Live together,

Due to stress and Depression,
Nowadays
Parents argue and
Get problems by blaming each other and go to the courts
And take diverse,

While parents see
The smile
Of child, they would
Like to withdrawal their petitions and
Compromise each Other and continue
Their lives joyfully,

The smile of child can
Change the lives of
Many parents to be
Alive and happy in
This world.

Raja Das

I am Raja Das from Jamshedpur,
Working as Service Executive in Tata Motors,
Reading is my hobby and writing too.

Dear Krishna

Dear Krishna,
I say I am the king of my life without have control in my own mind.
I say I am a satisfied man with thousands of needs.
I say I am the best without comparing to all.
I say I am educated just with very few certificates in the file.
I say I have a bright future even I can't see the next step.
I say I am happy and finding it in another thought.
I say I am in love without belief.
I say I am looking great with a poor heart.
I say I love nature by destroying it.
I say I am successful by spoils people's dreams.
I say I am socially connected without knowing about my neighbors.
I say I am a religious person and go to temples to beg my needs.

Just prove me wrong and enlighten me to be a human with humanity.

Aastha Gulati

आस्था गुलाटी स्वर्गीय श्री राजेश कुमार की सुपुत्री है। उनकी माता श्रीमती रजनी वाणिज्य की अध्यापिका है। उनका जन्म 12 **अप्रैल** 2004 पानीपत में हुआ था। उन्होंने दसवीं की परीक्षा सीबीएसई बोर्ड से करी है। उनकी रूचि लिखने व नृत्य पर है।

दास्तान पहली मुलाकात की!!

पहली मुलाकात जिसमें थी अलग सी बात
वो शर्माती नज़रे और कांपते हुए हाथ
उफ़!!! तेरा वो झुकी पलकों से छुप कर देखना
कुछ जादू था उस पल में मैंने भी ये माना
वो पहली मुलाकात जिसमें थी अलग सी बात

वो हमारी आंखों का पहली बार मिलना
वो हमारे हाथों का पहली बार टकराना
वो मेरा सर तेरे कांधे पर पहली बार रखना
वो मेरी जुल्फों के साथ तेरा पहली बार खेलना
वो पहली मुलाकात जिसमें थी अलग सी बात

वो तेरी अनरुकी बातें और मेरा तुझे लगातार देखना
उफ़!!! वो तेरा मुझसे भी ज्यादा शर्माना
वो तेरा हाथ आगे बढ़ाना और जिंदगी भर का साथ मांगना
वो तेरा मुझे पहली बार जान कहकर बुलाना
वो पहली मुलाकात जिसमें थी अलग सी बात

वो आखिर में हमारा फिर अलविदा कहना
वो आंखों में फिर मिलने की आस लेकर जाना
वो मुझे जाते देख तेरा 'सुनो ना' कहकर बुलाना
वो आखिर में तेरा फिर प्यार का इकरार करना
हाय!!! वो पहली मुलाकात जिसने थी अलग सी बात
जिसमें थी अलग सी बात.....

Diksha

Diksha is from Rohtak, Haryana. **She's pursuing M.Sc Mathematics** from **Sh. L.N. Hindu College, Rohtak.** Apart from being a poetess and a writer she is also a theatre artist.

<u>मैं हूं यहां, तुम हो कहां,</u>

मैं हूं यहां, तुम हो कहां,
ढूंढे मेरी नजर अब तुम को हर जगह।
यह रात हसीन, हसीन यह समा,
मैं हूं यहां तुम हो कहां।

देखो इस चांद को ,चांदनी बिखराए हुए हैं,
तुम आओगे इसी आस में,
हम रास्ते पर नजरें गड़ाए हुए हैं।
महसूस करो यह ठंडी हवा, जो तन से मेरे लिपट के जाए,
कभी मुझे तंग करे,
कभी तुम्हारा एहसास दे जाए।
इस चांदनी में मदहोश हूं मैं,
तुम भी आकर मदहोश हो जाओ।
तुझ में मैं खोऊ , तुम मुझ में खो जाओ।

तुम्हारी यादों का सहारा लेकर अब मन आवारा फिरता है,
तेरा अक्स देखकर बार-बार फिर तेरे प्यार में गिरता है,
यह सर्द हवाएं मेरे रोम रोम को इश्क से भर जाती है,
फिर मेरे जिस्म को तेरे जिस्म की मांग और बढ़ जाती है।
अधूरी रातें, अधूरी कुछ बातें, अधूरी मुलाकाते भी पूरी करनी है,
अब आजा ए सनम, मेरे दिल की खाली जगह भी तुमको ही भरनी है।
मैं हूं यहां, तुम हो कहां,
ढूंढे मेरी नजर तुम्हें अब हर जगह।

अजनबी

हां, हम अजनबी है
अनजाने इस जहां में ,
एक दूसरे से अजनबी।
पर कहते हैं कि कोई बेवजह नहीं मिलता,
किसी से मिलने की एक वजह होती है।
हम मिले हैं,
तो वजह भी जरूर होगी।
शायद आज नहीं तो कल राहें भी एक होंगी,
किस्मत का क्या कहूं,
वह तो कभी भी पलट जाए।
जो आज साथ है,
शायद कल को जुदा भी हो जाए।
थोड़ा तुम भरोसा करना,
थोड़ा हम कर लेंगे,
एक-एक कदम चल कर यह फासले भी कम कर लेंगे।
परत दर परत अपने आप को खोलेंगे,
जो इस जहां से छुपाया था,
वह राज़ एक दूसरे को बोलेंगे।
कुछ तुम आगे बढ़ना,
कुछ हम आगे बढ़ेंगे,
थोड़ा तुम मुझे सुनना,
थोड़ा हम तुमको सुनेंगे ।
साथ का वादा किए,
बगैर साथ निभाएंगे,
दो अनजाने एक होकर,
इस दुनिया से अनजाने हो जाएंगे।

Kapil Sahare

Kapil Sahare is **a Civil Engineer by profession and Writer by passion.** He is hailing from Bhopal (MP) and graduated from **UIT RGPV** Bhopal. He is a humble and generous person who loves to write his own words what he has within. He is also **a Poet, a Novelist, a Nature Lover and an enthusiast** contributing to Welfare Works. He's certain that he has the power to change lives for the better. It is his own way to keep himself sane, happy and in love with life. He himself is a practitioner of Vipassana meditation, which constantly inspires him to learn something new, strive for learning and personal development.

Insta id: @kapilsahare01

चलो इसे इस तरह से समझा जाए

शिकार- मुझे भी सुशांत, रिया, कगंणा की तरह TRP चाहिए।

दोषी- बहन, तु इन चक्करो मे ना पड।

शिकार- अरे, तुम सोचो तो, कितना मीडिया आएगा गांव मे, नाम होगा, आमदनी बढेगी।

दोषी- हम हाथ जोडकर विनती करते हैं, भगवान से ड़रो।

शिकार- पूरा देश देखेगा की एक लड़की के लिए छोटे साहब एकदम धांसू वाला ट्रीट करेंगे। बड़े साहब 18 घंटे काम करते थक जाएंगे, इसलिए वो नही कर पाएंगे।

दोषी- हमें समाज की लाज रखनी हैं।

शिकार- लाज ? ये क्या होता हैं?

दोषी- बहन, तू ज़िद मत कर। चल साथ मे उठेंगे, बैठेंगे, खाना खाएंगे और मिलजुलकर रहेंगे।

शिकार- अरे मूर्खों, भगवान से ड़रो। ऐसा करने से तुम्हे पाप लगेगा, पाप।

दोषी- नही, नही बहन, हमें बक्श दो।

शिकार– सुनो, आप सभी लोग आओ और ड़रो मत।

दोषी- नही, नही, हमें नही खेलना।

शिकार- सुनो, खेलना सेहत के लिए अच्छा होता हैं। मेरे जीते जी आप लोग खेलो, उसके बाद मेरी लाश के साथ होस्पिटल, पुलिस, शासन-प्रशासन सब खेलेंगे।

दोषी– हम कुछ समझे नही बहन।

शिकार- देखो, पहले मैं खुद ही अपने-आप लाचार-बेबस हो जाऊंगी, फिर होस्पिटल वालो को ढंग से इलाज ही नही करने दुंगी, फिर मजाक-मजाक मे मरने का नाटक करूँगी, फिर घरवालो के बगैर ही रात मे अपने आप को जलवाऊंगी।

दोषी– अरे, अरे, एक मिनट रुक जा बहन, रुक जा। हिन्दू रिती के अनुसार रात मे नही जला सकते।

शिकार- तुम भी बेवकुफ ही हो। अरे, मेरे साथ खेलोगे, तो सभी को पता चल जाएगा ना।

दोषी- लेकिन पोस्टमॉर्टेम रिपोर्ट का क्या ?

शिकार- सुनो, पहले तो मैं मरते-मरते गलत बयान दुंगी, फिर भी अगर डॉ. ना माने और सही रिपोर्ट लिखी, तो मैं ही चुपके से उसे बदल दुंगी, अब ठीक हैं।

दोषी- लेकिन अगर भारतीय जाग गए और आंदोलन करेंगे तो..?

शिकार- उसके लिए छोटे साहब से आग्रह करके मैं पूरा पुलिस फोर्स अपने गांव के चारो तरफ लगवा दुंगी, ताकि कोई दिक्कत ना हो ।

दोषी- लेकिन लोग फिर भी न माने तो..?

शिकार- जब कोर्ट मे साबित ही नही हो पाएगा, तो क्या कर लेंगे सब लोग? आखिर संविधान और न्यायालय नाम की भी कोई चीज हैं य़ा नही हैं इस देश मे?

दोषी- लेकिन बहन, तेरे घरवाले अगर ना माने तो..?

शिकार- हा उनका कुछ सोचना पढ़ेगा। अम्म.. फिर ऐसा करुँगी, बड़े साहब से मिन्नत करूँगी की जब स्तिथी बद-से-बदतर होने को आए, तो अपने व्यस्त समय मे से थोड़ा समय निकाल के रोना गाना, भाषण बाजी कर देंगे, तो बड़ा उपकार होगा हम पर।

दोषी- सुनो भाइयो, मम्मी ने गर्मा-गरम जलेबी बनाई हैं घर मे, चलो।

शिकार- अरे सुनो.. रुको.. ठीक हैं, चले जाओ। अब मैं ही खुद अपने साथ खेल लेती हूँ और सारी TRP भी मैं ही लूँगी, समझे।

Sabeera Nowreen

Sabeera Nowreen hails from the city of Guwahati in Assam. She **graduated** from **Bangalore University** with triple majors in **Psychology, Zoology and Botany.** Sabeera is an ardent admirer of poetry and prose however; she began to write poetry 3 years ago and has contributed to several anthologies till date. She believes that writing is amazingly cathartic. And that's why she is attached to it more than anything.

(1)
A PRESENT FROM STARS

I sat alone quietly
And gazed at the sky above me.
The clouds travelled by
And so swirled the brook of memories.
It was hazy and dark,
At times it felt like an old abandoned park.
Till something sparked thick yet merry in the sky
And the air brings to me my missing piece.
God exists now that I don't deny!

This magical place is a waterfront,
Or is a long stretch of swaying greens?
All I can see is a dark spread,
And a star shooting down to the position I have been.
Along with that does the air approaches my senses, confiding
me...
"Here is your missing piece
And now you can breathe in peace.
Here is your wish, your brother,
Take care, coz he's is gonna be forever!"

To My Dear Love Of That Time...

The control was yours;
Yet the soul remains mine.
If I point on the deeds during that reign,
You might not believe in the divinity of the sunshine.

It is indeed personal;
In which, the person is me.
I had kept you blanketed inside my warm velvety sky,
Till you distorted my sense of "We".

Barsha Das

She is born to save lives what her father used to says. She does that but she needs to survive first and **poetry is the food she needs for her life.** Don't worry if you ever get drenched by her soft drizzling poetry you won't catch a cold, she makes sure of that.

A Surreal Connection

Sometimes I think
I love you,
because you aren't mine
I love you
because you are far hundreds of miles

Sometimes I think
I love you
because we can't be together
and time won't get any jealousy to fight for

Sometimes I think
I love you,
because I can't hold you
as so there won't be possibilities to lose you

Sometimes I think
I love you,
because there's no trap
and also there's no escape

Sometimes I think
in this uncertain life, my love for you is forever.

All that I wish

I wish I were a flower
I could have offered myself
In your morning prayer

 I wish I were a dream catcher
 I could have removed all your bad dreams
 through me ,making them filter

I wish I were a candle
I could have brighten up your room
when you have a dark night to handle

 I wish I were a star
 I could have fallen for you
 to fulfil all your wishes and polish your scar

But I am only a human
 this life has given me "you"
and so much love for you
so I am proud ,for what I am

Dharmesh Sinha

धर्मेश सिन्हा वर्तमान में बैंक ऑफ इंडिया में मुख्य कैशियर के पद पर कार्यरत हैं। लेकिन वह अपने लेखन के माध्यम से अपने विचारों को व्यक्त करने में सबसे अधिक रुचि रखते हैं।

प्रेम प्रसंगों पर लिखना, एक बौद्धिक दिमाग होना, जिसमे जीवन की दुविधा और सच्चाई का पता लगाने की गहरी इच्छा होना, इनकी प्रमुख खासियत रही है।

यादें तेरी

आज फिर उसी राह से गुजरे
जिस राह पर कभी हम मिलते थे
लोगों की नजरों से छुप कर
जहां एक दूसरे को बांहों में रहते थे
आज फिर यादें तेरी दिल को दस्तक दे रही है
आज फिर ये राहें मुझसे तेरे बारे में पूछ रही है
रूप को तेरे छुप छुप के जुगनू भी निहारते थे
मिल के तुमसे हम तो जैसे जीते थे
बिछड़े तुमसे अब एक ज़माना हो गया
यादें तेरी दिल में मेरे अब एक तराना बन गया
गुनगुना रहे थे मिल के जो गीत कभी
अब वो मेरे जीने का बहाना बना गया

Ratnesh Paras Singh

My name is Ratnesh Singh. I love to Read and write shayari. I want to do something different and I am dreamer and want to live a healthy lifestyle. I have Written some lines on **"PYAAR ME KUSHI aur GHAM**. I hope you all will like this.

Pyaar Me Khushi Aur Gham

Maine tumse pyaar kiya aur tum bewafa ho gayi,
Main khush tha tumhe paake aur tum door ho gayi,
Kya khata ho gayi humse jo mili mere dil ko aisi saja,
Hum tumhe dil me basane lage aur tum kisi aur ke dil me bas
gayi.

Mere dil me jagah bana ke tum kisi aur ki ho gayi,
Mere pyaar me kya kami hui jo tum bewafa ho gayi,
Tumhaari bewafaayi itni dard de gayi mere dil me,
Hum tum pe marte rahe aur tum maut de gayi,
Kabhi koi kehta hain message na karna,
Kabhi koi kehta hain call na karna,
Hum hi intazaar karte reh jaate hain unke call aur message ki,
Phir wo kehte hain ki aap hamari chahat na karna.

Manga maine us vidhata se apne sapno ki pari,
Tumhe jo dekha pehli dafa tum direct dil me utari,
Aaj bhi teri wo addayein meri khushi ki kaaran ban jati hain,
Sun li vidhata ne meri fariyaade tum meri taqdeer me aa
mili,

Pyaar ke har pal ko maine tumse hi jana hain,
Pyaar me kya sukoon hain maine tumse hi jana hain,
Tumne hi to seekhaya hain mujhe pyaar ka matalab kya hota
hain,
Jab bhi maine pyaar ki zikra ki hain tumhaara hi naam aaya
hain...

Teri zulfen aise lehraaye mera dil chura le jaaye,
Teri ankhiyon ki nazar aise dekhe mujhe ghayal kar jaaye,
Tera wo cute sa smile jiska main deewana hua,

Jis shabd ko sunane ke liye bekaraar hain mera dil wo tere
lafzo se baya ho jaaye...

Tu apni zulfen lehraa ke pyaar se uthaye mujhe main us pal
ka intazaar karta hu,
Har subah me main tere hathon ki us coffiee ka intazaar karta
hu,
Kabhi sheeshen ki jaraurat na pade apni khubshurti dekhne
ke liye,
Main tere har wo khubshurti ki tareef karne ka intazaar karta
hu...

Apne pyaar ke har khubshurti ko gaur se dekhne do zara,
Meri dilruba mere samne baitho tumhaari tareef karne do
zara,
Main tujhe hamesha niharu tere us chand se bhi khubshurat
chehre ko,
Apni nasili aankhon ke samandar me mujhe doob jaane do
zara

Dr. Rakesh R Mund

Dr Rakesh R Mund has been participating in more than **150 anthologies** and his solo books are **Ishq-e-panhi & Vidhwansh** available on Amazon, Flipkart and others platform. He is winner of **OMG BOOK OF RECORDS.** He read Veda and diffrent literatures which give a glimpse on his writing.

IG: @Rakeshmundr_

<u>हिज्र</u>

हिज्र के रात उम्र भी मांगा था मैं
वो बोलती रही सबकुछ गुंगा था मैं

नजर पड़ते ही उसने नजर बचाया
बदलती रही वो रंग ,एक-रंगा था मैं

धड़कन को धड़काके धड़कना छोड़ा
वो सफेद खून वाली और पिंगा था मैं

हरकतों से कहाँ वो पता चलती थी
वो दादर के स्टेशन और माटुंगा था मैं

नक्श-ए-उल्फ़त भी मिट गया अब
वो रंग छोड़ती कपडा और तिरंगा था मैं

अहद-ए-शबाब को क्या बताता **"राकेश"**
वो गलियों के बहती पानी और गंगा था मैं

तुम्हें मालूम नहीं

पत्थर फैंकने को तयार जमाने वाले
तुम्हें मालूम नहीं
शीशे कि बदन तुम्हारी देखते प्याले
तुम्हें मालूम नहीं

करवटें ले रही है किसमत कभी भी पलट सकती है
गोरे मुखड़े पे मत देखो बदन है काले
तुम्हें मालूम नहीं

जाम छलकाए शाम रंगीन करेंगे अपने काम के लिए
फर्जी इश्क़ में अश्क़ दिखाने वालेतुम्हें मालूम नहीं

नमाज पढ़ेंगे प्रार्थना करेंगे केंडल जलाके माथा टेकेंगे
जब दंगे होंगे करेंगे पंगे तुम्हारे हवाले
तुम्हें मालूम नहीं

धूप में खड़ा होकर "राकेश" बारिश की बात मत कर
इन्द्रधनुष नहीं दिखता रात में लाले
तुम्हें मालूम नहीं

Megha P. Yadav

Megha P. Yadav, born and brought up in the hills of Meghalaya. She's a student, an author and a social worker. She has been a part of more than seventy anthologies including **20+ record holding anthologies.** She has been feathered in National Magazines like **Taare Zameen Par** and has published her work in some international magazines too. She has compiled more than **5 national and international anthologies** some of them are **"Panphysicm #we too feel", "Wings of falcon", Garden of Wild Roses", "Sapiens become Seprants", "In the year 2020"** etc. Moreover, she a **national level debator** and has been a part of record holding 24+ hours longest debate competition. Moreover, she is the state representative and manager of **"Horn Ok Please"** team (an open mic event organisation).

Do Short Clothes Describe One's Character?

Shorts dresses makes me feel comfortable, and if your eyes find it wrong or uncomfortable it's your issue not mine! Some say's- "Beta, wear decent clothes, this doesn't look good on you." These are suggestion form those people who always has indecent topics to talk about. I wear shorts pants, crop tops and yes, sometimes my cleavage is also seen. But, I don't wear it to attract anyone, I wear it because summer's is hot and shots are light and comfortable. Some people say that girls were shorts to pull boys attentions and than when they are raped these girls blame boys. I too question to such people that when boys were short pants do they also wear to attract girls or do girls rape or abuse them after seeing in shorts?

It's my choice to choose they way I dress. I don't dress for someone else; I dress according to my will and for myself. In short, my shorts aren't as short as your mentality dear judgemental people. My shorts aren't the cruse of the society but your way of thinking and looking at someone is!

Er. Mohit A. Arya

Mohit name itself states impression of other. Being an Engineer he is a writer by heart.

Ensnarled by beauty of his writing, the words by hearth he wants to share some messages from his view.

A boy who lives in the beauty of viewing the world with different aspect of seeking the world with different angle of imagination.

As a writer he only expresses his feelings in the word seeking the situation of the world. He is having a single wish to give other way or imagination to seek the world with his eye.

IG: @nature_nuts_1
Facebook id: Monu A. Arya

सफ़र

तुमसे ही शुरूआत सफ़र की
तुम्हारे साथ अंत भी,
तुमसे ही निर्मित है
यह सारी सृष्टि।

तुमने ही वजूद बनाया है,
तुमने ही ये जग चलाया है,
तुम में है ताक़त वो दर्द सहने की,
जिससे इस संसार में नया जीवन आया है।

अगर तुम न हो तो
ये संसार कैसे बढ़ेगा,
अगर तुम न हो तो
ये संसार कैसे चलेगा,

यूं तो दुनिया करती है बोहोत ज़ुल्म तुम पर
फिर भी तुम्ही हो निर्माता-ए-जीवन सबका,
तुम न हो तो ये संसार कैसे चलेगा,
तुम बिन ये जग कुछ नहीं कुछ नहीं

यहाँ दुनिया में प्यार का वजूद तुमसे ही,
यहाँ दुनिया में धर्म की उत्पत्ति तुमसे ही,
यहाँ धन की उत्पत्ति तुम्हारा ही वजूद है,
यहाँ जो भी है सब तुमसे ही है,
तुम बिन ये जग कुछ नहीं कुछ नहीं,

तब भी क्यों ये संसार तुम पर ज़ुल्म ढाता है ,
क्यों ये तुम्हारे वजूद को गर्भ में मारता है,

मेरा वजूद भी तुमसे है और दुनिया भी तुमसे ही,
तुम बिन ये जग कुछ नहीं कुछ नहीं,

क्यों घर के बेटी सब सेहती रहे,
जब के उसके पढ़ने से ही जग की उन्नति है ।

घर के बेटी को,
सबकी बेटी को ये जग क्यों घूरता है ,
घर चलाने को भी,
जरूरी स्त्री का होना है.
प्रेमिका तो सभी को होना है
पर फिर भी घर पर बेटी नहीं होना है,
क्या होगा अगर वो पढ़ जाएगी
सिर्फ यही होगा की वो घर संसार अच्छा चलाएगी,
क्यों उसपर इतने अत्याचार होते है,
हरदिन कितने लड़कियो से यु बलत्कार होते है।

पर उसने भी इन्ही को सबसे बड़ा जन्म का अधिकार अर्पण किया है,
यु तो वो बनता है सबकी किस्मत
पर यह वो व्यक्ति है जो ईश्वर से अपने हक्क के लिए लड़ जाती है और भी कर जाती है,
जैसे कि सावित्री ने छीने थे अपने पति के प्राण यमराज से वैसे ही ताकत इन सभी में है.
फिर भी संसार इनपे ही जुल्म ढाता है .
जिनके बिना ये कुछ नहीं कुछ नहीं

तुम हो तो सब है
तुम बिन ये दुनिया कुछ नहीं
कुछ नहीं

कुछ नहीं

आप ही रूप हो मर्दानी का
आप ही रूप हो राधा का
आप ही रूप हो शक्ति का
आप ही रूप हो लक्ष्मी का
आप ही रूप हो धरती माँ का
आप ही माँ जगदम्बा
आप ही रूप हो देव पार्वती का
आप ही हो धरोहर विद्या का
आप ही रूप हो देवी सरस्वती की

अगर तुममे तो कुछ नहीं,
कुछ नहीं

तुम बिन ये जग है एक कालिख अँधियारे का शिकार
तुम बिन ये जग कुछ नहीं कुछ नहीं

Kameshvar Verma

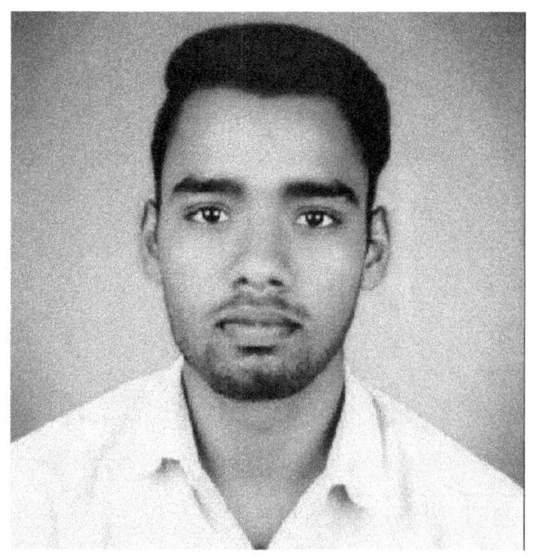

Kameshvar Verma is a civil engineer by profession. He likes writing, reading and listening Hindi poems. He shares his thoughts and life experiences by lines, poetry and Shayari.
Follow him on:
Instagram: @kameshvar_verma
Your quote: @kamesh_verma1011
Email: kamesh.verma1011@gmail.com

मां

वो बड़े दिनों बाद आई, मैंने सारी बेचैनी खो दिया,
मेरी "मां" मुस्कुराई, और मैं रो दिया...

Memories of College Life

सुबह हो या शाम लिखो, दिन हो या रात लिखो,
Whenever you're free, दिल की बात लिखो,
ग़म के बादल से, खुशी की बरसात लिखो,
जिंदगी के हालात लिखो, ना अपने जज़्बात लिखो,
कॉलेज की वो याद लिखो, छोटी बड़ी हर बात लिखो,
शुरुआत के दिनों में, घर की वो याद लिखो,
छुट्टियों पर घर जाने की, उत्सुकता वाली रात लिखो,
गुरुवार के भंडारे में, मिली वह प्रसाद लिखो,
चाय की टपरी पे, यारों की मुलाकात लिखो,
एग्जाम की टेंशन में, जागी हर रात लिखो,
असाइनमेंट और प्रोजेक्ट में, दोस्तों का वो साथ लिखो,
छोटी-बड़ी गलतियों पे, मैडम कि वो डांट लिखो,
कैरियर के मार्गदर्शन में, टीचर का वो साथ लिखो,
कविता या शायरी में ना सही,
अपने ही शब्दों में अपनी बात लिखो...

ऐ मेरे बचपन

ऐ मेरे बचपन...!
तेरे निशान ढूंढता हूं...
जहां पूरी फैमिली रहा करते थे एक ही रूम में,
मैं वो छोटा सा मकान ढूंढता हूं।
अनेकों खेल खेला उन गलियों में, कंचे, भौंरे, आदि,
मैं वो सारा सामान ढूंढता हूं।
दो रूपए लेकर जाया करते थे जिस चौराहे पर,
मैं वो छोटा सा दुकान ढूंढता हूं।
मेरी नादान सी बातों से मम्मी-पापा के चेहरे पर,
मैं वो प्यारी सी मुस्कान ढूंढता हूं।
दुनिया कि बातों से बेखबर और अनजान,
मैं खुद में वो नादान ढूंढता हूं।
ऐ मेरे बचपन...!
तेरे निशान ढूंढता हूं

"The beauty of soul, mind and behavior creates an image inside any human being that never fades."

Manisha Singh

BPT Student, Love for poetry and singing.
Aimed at bringing something better.
Navodayan.
A proud Bihari.

(1)

My past looks like
A unique scenery to me everytime.
I often open the windows and look at it for hours
gazing at corners left undiscussed.
I find my smiles floating on the waves
that enfolded my past.
I often delve deeper to find answers.
Pain that was camouflaged by still so fresh tinge of sky's
blue.
It has vines that swathed some unuttered stories.
I could see my allies, how the colors could mingle to sketch
and dye me into life.
I could count every single moment
That wove its wings to be my sky.
I was thrilled one time, agonized another second.
And I pulled the shimmery curtains together,
breathing deep...in contentment.
Cherished and well embellished some pasts,
teach us why we should live the happiest
In each second.
When I forget my ways,
I will come to you again.
But for now let's be the life in hue of present.

(2)

वो नज़र तेरी कुछ ऐसी
वो नज़र तेरी कुछ ऐसी थी,
बारिश को जैसे बादल था। ×2
कुछ बिखरे-बिखरे तुम से थे,
कुछ सिमटा-सिमटा मुझसा था।
वो नज़र तेरी कुछ ऐसी थी,
जैसे फूलों को इश्क़ धूप से था।
एक ओर झुका आस्माँ था,
एक ओर उठी धरती भी थी। ×2
जाने क्या दिखा था उसमें,
जाने क्यूँ भीड़ में जुदा-सा था।
वो नज़र तेरी कुछ ऐसी थी,
रेत में जैसे आबसार था।
मौसम बेशक कोई ज़रीफ़ था,
ये हवा उसकी ज़रीफ़ा थी।×2
वो नज़र तेरी कुछ ऐसी थी,
हर दरिया को जैसे साहिल था।
वो नज़र तेरी कुछ ऐसी थी,
बारिश को जैसे बादल था।
बारिश को जैसे बादल था।

Vanshika Gupta

Vanshika Gupta
Grown in Moga, Punjab
Love to write and travel.

Life

Life is not easy, life is not meant for it
You have to pay for everything here,
Your smile cost u as well as your cry,
If you want something you like,
You need to sacrifice something you love,
Life is not easy, life is not meant for it.

If you are sad it relief your pain,
If you are happy it cherish your day,
But life not gives what you want,
But what you deserve,
Life is not easy, life is not meant for it

Life is meant for give and take,
Give your hard work and take your happiness,
It never stops,
But there is a stop, but it cost your life
Death is the end which never lies,
Death is what life is meant for.

Life is not easy, life is not meant for it

Some More Words

Everyone say that a morning is a new start
But I say it's just to continue the same path
It's just another day in your life
Bringing happiness and sorrow
Giving you experience or telling you some harsh truth
Making you sad or giving you expectation
Your today is link with your past
And your present becomes a past in future
So there will always a tomorrow
Always a yesterday
And always a present
Past becomes memories
Memories make our future
just go on with the same path in every morning with some twist of direction
Giving essence to your present
So every morning is a new start of same path.

Vedika Bhoot

Vedika Bhoot was **born in 2005** in a small town near Durgapur, West Bengal. She mostly **writes free verse poetry and often entwines fiction around reality.** The themes of her poem are drawn from her own life experiences. She believes in investing time to construct and live a world within oneself as much as one does for the world outside. This newly developed bud aspires to bloom into a well groomed flower in the eternal garden of poetry.

The Pencil

A pencil I was
Tall, lean and confident
A dull grey lead crowning my base
Sharpened finely to a delicate point
Over crisp white sheets
That lay undisturbed beneath the book cover

I scribled over the sheets
Undefined lines meeting the gleaming white stretches
Each page coming out with a whole new design
With lines not straight and shades not perfect
But the picture bearing a picture of my heart

And on one fine page
I met a pen
With a sunshine yellow colour
who left her book to fill mine
To fill colours in my dull grey book
To help my scribbles turn into drawings.

And together we left a bicoloured trail
Moving in perfect synchronisation
Sheets after sheets
Perfect pictures of yellow and grey
With straight lines and brilliant shades
The shining yellow complemented my dull grey

And on another fine page
She changed her colours
Or maybe showed the colours she truly carried
Leaked those colours on me and my sheets
Inked all the beautiful pictures that seemed a masterpiece

Stained many sheets that awaited to be drawn over
And left forever the trail of her bleeding colours

What was I to do now?
Those beautiful pictures behind haunted me
The inked sheets ahead dampened my spirits
"My beautiful book" was no more beautiful and no more mine
Time ran fast, recovery went slow
Repenting for the yellow glow.

Down I looked the book smiled back
Still the same bright smile
that he had when I completed my first page
He held me tight and showed me through his eyes
The hundred pages that still lay to be drawn over.

"Are those stains stronger than your dreams?
You still are the tall, lean confident pencil,
who can scribble out his heart over the white sheets
who can still create wonders with the beautiful grey.
So redraw those stains into beautiful designs
Knit memorable stories in those bare pages"

And on that fine page
"My beautiful book" was again mine.

Babita Goel

मैं बबीता गोयल हरिद्वार की निवासी हूँ| मैंने **M.Com** किया है| मुझे लिखना इसलिए पसंद है क्योंकि लिखना एक आत्मिक अनभूति है जो हम शब्दो को लिख कर व्यक्त कर सकते है और मुझको अवसर मिला तो मैं **नारी शोषण**, rishte, **समाज, राजनेता** जैसे विषयो पर प्रकाश डालना चाहूंगी | मुझको सच्ची घटनायो पर आधारित विषयो पर रुबरु करना यही प्रयास है मेरा|

नारी शक्ति

नारी तेरे असंख्य रूप है
कभी माँ लक्ष्मी, सरस्वती तो कभी
माँ दुर्गा का अवतार है
झांसी की रानी सी वीरता तुझमें,
मीरा सा प्रेम पाया है
मदर टेरेसा ने दीन दुखियों के,
जीवन को चमकाया है
तुम इस युग की अबला नारी हो,
इंद्रा-सरोजिनी जैसी हस्तियां बन
राष्ट्र के गौरव को बढ़ाये हो,
सीता जैसी पावन बन संस्कृति का मान बढ़ाये हो
नारी शक्ति तुझे इस कठिन मंच पर,
सर्वोच्च स्थान पर नवाजा है
पुरुष प्रधान समाज की बेड़ियों को तोड़,
बुलंदियो को छूना है
समाज के इन थकेदारो की परवाह ना कर आगे बढ़ना है
सर्वश्रेष्ठ देकर देश का गौरव बढ़ाना है
नारी तुम शक्ति हो अबला हो
जग जननी हो श्रृष्टि निर्माता हो
तुम अदभुत कृति हो ईश्वर की,
हर मार्ग पर अग्रसर हो
नवीन युग का निर्माण कर
अपने सपने साकार करो
नारी शक्ति अपना जीवन सार्थक करो
हर मंजिल पर फतह करो
नारी शक्ति तेरा सम्मान हो
तेरी जय जय कार हो

बिहारी जी

हे बिहारी जी मेरा रिश्ता पर्दे में ही रखना,
इस दुनिया की नजरो से सदा बचाये रखना।
मेरी वाणी हमेशा तेरा गुणगान करे,।
तेरे मनमोहक रूप का दीदार करे,
हे मेरे ठाकुर जगत के सब रिश्तों को तुझमें पाया,
तेरी करुणा ने जीवन का पाठ पढाया।
शानो शौकत हो ऐसी बनु बेहसहारो का सहारा,
तेरे नाम के स्मरण बिना ना हो मेरा गुजारा।
मेरे लबो पर हमेशा तेरा नाम रहे,
मैं सुख दुख में रहु, हृदय में सदा तेरा वास रहे
हे सर्व शक्तिमान नाजुक बंधन को पर्दे में रखना,
तेरे पतित पावन रूप के दर्शन कर निहाल हो
जाऊ में, मन ही मन अपने भाग्य पर इत्राउ में,
मेरे ठाकुर सेठ अपनी भक्ति में गोता लगाने दे
मन में सदा करुणा का भाव रहे,
तु मुझमे है मैं तुझमें हुँ इस गुप्त रिश्ते का मान रहे

Saloni Lal Srivastava

She is Saloni Lal Srivastava daughter of Mr. Kumar Prashant and Mrs. Asha Sinha from Siwan, Bihar.
She is currently, working as a Project Coordinator under Flairs & Glairs Publication House.
And also, **pursuing B.Sc in Botany honours**.
Her life is all around her family, friends and career.
She has also worked as co author in **50+ anthologies.**
She is the one who loves to spread smile and positivity to everyone.
You can follow her on Instagram:
@salonilalsrivastava.

ख्वाब

ख्वाब,
जिससे मन की खूबसूरती झांकती,
जिसको नहीं जरूरतें बाँधती,
जिसपे किसी का न चलता है जोर,
जो अँधेरी रातों को भी कर दे भोर,
उसी ख्वाब का अब होना है हमको,
उसी ख्वाब को जीना है वर्षों।

ख्वाब,
जिसको शिकायत नहीं लम्हों से,
जिसमें सिफारिश नहीं औरों से,
जो हसरतों के है जहाज सजाता,
जो टूट कर फिर से है जीना सिखाता।
उसी ख्वाब का होना है हमको,
उसी ख्वाब में खोना है हमको।हाँ वही ख्वाब,
जिसपर न बस मेरा न तुम्हारा,
पर जिसमें हो जग सारा हमारा,
उसी ख्वाब में अब जीते है हम,
और उसी ख्वाब को अब मरते है हम।
हो एक हकीकत और वही ख्वाब हो,
ऐसी ही कोशिश अब हर बार हो।

शिक्षा

शिक्षा जरूरी है इतनी
चाहिए जितनी खाने की रोटी
सारे काँटों की जड़ है अशिक्षा
क्यों नहीं समझता तू यह बात छोटी

क्यों तुम्हारे ही बच्चे हैं भूखे ?
तन पर कपड़ा नहीं क्यों तुम्हारे ?
क्यों ठिठुरती है मइया तुम्हारी ?
बिन दवाई के बूढ़ा बाप बड़ा रे,
जो कमाते हो जाता कहा रे
क्यों ना जुटती है तन पर लंगोटी
शिक्षा जरूरी है इतनी
चाहिए जितनी खाने को रोटी

शिक्षा केवल खेल नहीं है
जान लो मात्र तुम पढ़ना लिखना
ये भी समझो कि दुनिया कहां है
अपनी पैरों पे कैसे खड़े हो
यह शिक्षा की अंतिम कसौटी
शिक्षा जरूरी है इतनी
चाहिए जितनी खाने को रोटी

Mrs. Anmol Kanungo

मैं श्रीमती अनमोल कानूनगो।
वैसे तो में काफी समय से लिख रही हूँ ,पर मेरी रचना पहली बार प्रकाशित हो रही हैं। आशा है आप सभी को पसंद आएगी। और आपका आशीर्वाद व स्नेह भरपूर मिलेगा।

तुम हो तो मैं हूँ

मेरे सिंदूर का नाम हो तुम,
मेरी पायल की झंकार ,चूड़ियों की खनक,
बिंदियां की लाली ,काले सूत्र की पुकार हो तुम।
मेरे लाल जोड़े का श्रृंगार हो तुम,
मेरे नाम का उपनाम हो तुम।
मेरा मान, आत्मसम्मान,पहचान हो तुम।
मेरी साँसों में बसे कृष्ण,शंकर,राम हो तुम,
मेरे हर व्रत,कथा का सार हो तुम।
मैं कहती हूँ तुम्हारे बिना जी नही सकती,
क्योंकि मेरा दिल,धड़कन, मेरी जान हो तुम।
मेरे योवन से जश का आधार हो तुम,
मेरे दुःखो से खुशियो का मार्ग तुम।
अब कैसे समझाऊ तुम्हे की मेरे जीवन के ठहरे नीर की धार हो
तुम।

तेरा साथ

आज तू भी होगा,ओर बेशुमार इश्क़ भी होगा,
इतने दिनों की दूरियों का पूरा हिसाब होगा।
कहेंगे तुझसे दिल की हर एक बात,
मेरी इतनी तन्हा रातों के बाद आज तेरा साथ भी होगा।
तुझसे कहेगे अपने सारे अरमान,
दिल मे जो सम्मान हैं वो बयां भी होगा।
कैसे कटे दिन,कैसी बीती राते तेरे बिन,
उन लम्हो का अंत भी आज होगा।
खुशी ज़ाहिर नही हो रही कि,
आज फिर से तेरा साथ होगा।

Ankul Mishra

Ankul Mishra belongs to heart of mountains Haldwani in Uttarakhand and is currently **pursuing his Bacholers degree from Bhimtal.**
He loves to observe the world through different inclinations and pour his experience into words. You can follow him up on his socials to become a part of his family.

Instagram: @ankulmishra
YourQuote:
https://www.yourquote.in/ankul-mishra-5tep/quotes

(1)

It's normal to feel upsurged and stretched
the things that you're dreaming are a lill farfetched
you might not be clear about the vision that you have
towards the endpoint maturity is all that you grab
you're goals my friend are the reflection of who you are
maybe love life kids or some beer at the bar
its not about fate its not about the earnings
it's more about your bag and you on this journey
coz life is not a race as generally people exaggerate
it's an amalgamation of love with a lill bit of hate
So open up your wings and get ready to fly
wont disclose your value up until you try
wanna grab the pun and have a hell lot of fun?
all you have to do is work till dawn this of the sun
But do make sure to enjoy the path too
at the end you'll be the person standing right next to you.

(2)

कुछ बातें हैं जो अनकही है
पर आज बताना जरूरी है
चलो मान लिया ना भेद है तुझमें
ना मुझमें है अक्स कोई
जो हो गुलाब की पंखी तुम
मैं भी तो हूं सूरजमुखी
तुम फसलों की जो साथी हो
तो वर्षा बन गिर जाऊंगा
गर देखो एक ही चक्षु से
ते मात में भी कहलाऊंगा
तुम इंद्रप्रस्थ का राजा बन
जहाँ परचम को लहरओगे
मै इश्वर रथ का साथी बन
वहां प्रेम वर्षा करवाऊंगा
भेद ना बाँटो मुझसे तुम
सत्य मै भी बतलाऊंगा
गर हाथ जो थामोगे मेरा
जीवन को स्वर्ग बनाऊंगा

Anjaly Sangeeth

Anjaly Sangeeth, alias Geethanjaly R is a banker in the godly city of Tamilnadu, Trichy. She has always spoken best through writing. She **started writing poems at the age of 15** and ended up publishing her collection of poems with the help of her grandfather, **a versatile writer**. One of her poem won her a **Kerala state award.** She published her debut novel **"The Ineffable blu".** This write up is just a peak into her world.

Smokefall

It's an annoyingly bright day with the crowd pushing us into the hissing slimy train, which pours down the tunnels and rises up to the scorching sun.

The whole compartment seems to be having a wonderful day with smiles flowing back and forth. The usual corner with barely no view outside, was taken today by a foriegner of dissimilar looks.

"No one sits there" shouted an old man who had the thinnest neck, I had ever seen.

Now that was a concern thrown at the stranger yet he rejected it with utter silence.

"That seat is not taken." another friendly lady threw her hands to the other end of the train. It was beaming with light, feeling like the glass was merely holding the lively day from getting in.

"Why should the day grow more and more brighter?" I murmured to myself and accepted the defeat.

The specs broke the light fragments into small rays, sending it straight at my saggy eyelids.

A dedicated singer shouted out to my wavering mind through wires, but it's just a child version of your stubborn self running to the abondoned door that you never wish to knock on.

"Stay away from that" I shoved the fist into my lap and looked up to find the foriegner sitting across me. Finally he succeeded at grabbing my attention from the door.

He kept staring at me like any other human being. That was almost not abnormal anymore; the burns do attract the inhumans.

"Why didn't you run up to the door?" His question pulled the door wide open, splashing in all the light that the day could give.

"What?" I cared less with a breathless soul. "He needed you."
All the forts that were built to guard the night on the Parler
Avenue, broke brick by brick as the world shifted back to
that foggy doorstep.
"Try harder!" He shouted through the only air hole that the
fire missed. "That's all we can. Sorry. Get away from the
wall. It is too late."
"But he is still in there, burning in pain." The men pulled me
far from the door that almost became invisible to the
darkness and fog. The train jolted a big thud among the
yellowish sunflower fields.
"Ajay!" the eyes squeezed out all the tears that were left in
them. "I should have been there." there was absolute silence
amidst the chaotic human world.
"It would be writhing to be alive." I brushed off the water
away, his eyes looked familiar now.
"Don't come back to that smoke fall again. I am not there
anymore."

Deval Tripathi

Deval Tripathi, a high-school **ICSE Board student** is a writer, poet and a speaker belongs to Distt. Kannauj of Uttar Pradesh.He is fond of reading various types of novels, listening and playing musical instruments, writing poems and short stories and won first prize in Inter-House Debate and writing Competition for the last two consecutive years and also a deep nature lover and also a mythistic person.

He is of sound mind and also the **CMD & CEO OF TAM PVT. LMT...**

देवल के ख़याल

"ज़िन्दगी, मुझे भी तो मौका दे रूठने का कभी,
हर बार मेरे हिस्से में ' मनाना ' ही क्यों आता है?
कभी मुझे कोई रहबर अकेला छोड़ दे,
हर बार मेरे साथ ये ज़माना क्यों आता है?
कर दी नोमाइश मैंने दर्द की हुकूमत में,
लेकिन फिर भी मेरे दर्द में फ़साना क्यों आता है?"

"हटा लो अंजुमन से हृदय को अपने सनम,
के वापस कभी हम इस राह पे न आएंगे।
बहुत भटक लिए तेरी आँखों के जंगल में,
के बंद कर लो पलकें अब हम घर जाएंगे।।"

"पूछो मत हमसे ऐ जाने जां हम क्या लिखते हैं,
हर गीत में तुम्हारी खुशी की दुआ लिखते हैं।
तुम समझो दिल फ़रेब है मरज़ी तुम्हारी,
हम तो हर नुक्ते में अपनी जां लिखते हैं।।"

"तुम बार-बार बस यही गुनाह करती हो,
जब प्यार नहीं तो क्यों इधर निगाह करती हो?
क़त्ल करना है तो यूँ कर दो मेरा,
क्यूँ तुम खंजर पे इल्ज़ाम धरती हो

<u>एक रोज़ हम जुदा हो जाएंगे</u>

"एक रोज हम जुदा हो जाएंगे,
ना जाने कहाँ खो जाएंगे. ।

तुम लाख पुकारोगे हम को......
पर लौट कर हम ना आयेंगे ।

थक हार के दिन के कामों से,
जब रात को सोने आओगे ।
देखोगे जब फोन को अपने,
पैगाम मेरा ना पाओगे ।
तब याद तुम्हें हम आयेंगे,

पर लौट कर हम ना आयेंगे ।
एक रोज ये रिश्ता टूटेगा,

दिल इतना ज्यादा टूटेगा...
फिर कोई ना हम से रूठेगा..

हम ना आखे खोलेंगे,
तुम से कभी ना बोलेंगे !

आखिर उस दिन तुम रो दोगे,
ऐ दोस्त मुझे तुम खो दोगे...

Deenbandhu Chauhan

I am 23 years old and I am a resident of **Shivrinarayan, Chhattisgarh** and I love walking and seeing the natural scenery, as well as I love being in solitude, away from this crowd of the city.

Mail: chauhandeenbandhu42@gmail.com
Instagram: @bandhu.639

छोटी सी आशा

बस कहना नही अब कुछ करके दिखाना है,
जो देखा है अपना उस मंजिल को पाना है।
कहने से मंजिल मिल नही जाती राही को कतरा कतरा
खून -पसीने का अब हमको बहाना है।
सपने रातों को नहीं,
बस आंखों से देखा जाना है।
इन सपनों को अब मुझे सच करके दिखाना है।
जिन -जिन ने चाहा मुझे रोकना ,
उनको रोक दिखाना है।
अपनी हारी बाजी को अब मुझे जीत दिखाना है ।
कब तक दूं खुद को धोका अब खुद पे भरोसा लाना है।
अपने खोए वजूद को अब फिर से वापस पाना है।
मांगी मैंने खुद से माफ़ी,
अब इस लायक भी बन जाना है।
जिस पर गर्व कर सकोगे तुम
वो मुकाम अब पाना है,
हौसला हो खुद पे तो कुछ नामुमकिन नहीं होता है
इसी हौसले को अब अपना हथियार बनाना है।
सोचना नही कुछ अब बस करते चले जाना है ,
अपनी हर कमज़ोरी को अपनी ताकत मुझे बनाना है।
इस दुनिया में खोया था पर अब आगे जाना है ,
जिसको पूरी दुनिया जाने ,वो पहचान अब बनाना है।।

आत्मा की इच्छा

ऐ जिंदगी तू भी बड़ी अजीब है ,
कभी बहुत दूर ,तो कभी बहुत करीब है।
तेरे नखरे भी देख ,बड़े ही लाजवाब हैं,
किसी के लिए हम हैं अच्छे ,
तो किसी के लिए बड़े ही खराब हैं !!
कोई है जो हमसे ही सिख ,हमे ही समझते हैं ।
क्या करें ,हम जैसे हैं ! ऐसे ही हैं ।
वैसे भी हमें सब थोड़ी समझ पाते हैं ।
 कभी - कभी तो लगता है , अब थक सा गया हूं ,
तो कभी लगता है ,कहीं गुम हो गया हूं ।
 फिर करता हूं खुद से सवाल मैं बहुत से ,
तब जाके लगता है ,गुम नहीं में अभी भी वहीं हूं !!
 कुछ लोग हैं जिनके लिए मैं खास हूं ,
जिसने मुझे थोड़ा अपनाया ,उसपे करता हूं मैं पूरा यकिन ।
ऐ जिंदगी तुझे और क्या चाहिए मुझसे कितना तड़पाएगा

Jaymin Shah

Jaymin Shah was born in **1987** in **Gujarat**. With a very positive attitude towards new learning he was growing up, he was fascinated with lots of writing skills, and this interest led to some early exposure to reading since he was drawn to stories related to **Emotions, Motivations and Adventures**. Later, **Mr. Jaymin**, who now teaches Literatures at the higher secondary schools, developed a passion for ideas. In **THE UNTOLD LOVE**, Jaymin explores the issue of how Love is unchangeable by introducing an ability to express the love and what happens if the love is not expressed. The THE UNTOLD LOVE is Mr. Jaymin's first book under **Subharambh Publication House**.

And the words are dedicated to his love **Rivaan** and **Shrihaan**.

Insta I'd: @jaymin1439

Success the Attitude

"Success is nothing but the combination of your Potential and Struggle"- Jaymin Shah

A success has lots of definitions, it changes from person to person, and the same can be used in different ways too. To achieve it we need to first accept what we are, what are we up to? That means we have to make our own definition of success first, and then start to work on it. It is not that thing that everyone will get it on the very first trial, because not all the trials are for fruits, some are for the path to success, we just have to be clear with what path we want to be on.

No one has that caliber to have a success without struggle, no will get all the achievements at the very first stage, so it can be said that the first stage are the introductions of all the success stories, and then the journey to success begins. Now when we are on the journey to reach success we should keep one thing in mind that we will not get success alone because success is always a team work, it might be directly or indirectly. We should not forget anyone who helped us in our journey; we have to take them with us till the destination.

When you are able to create your own success definition you are said to be on the path to success, now if you are not able to find the path to success then we have to build it, but the main question is how? So if you want to make a path first fix your goal, then aim towards it, target it, and work on it, to work on the path we have to gather all the information related to our Goal, so that it can be easy to reach.

Lots of people have seen the success but among them some has fallen down, not because they didn't worked more but because they have changed the attitude towards work after

their success, so again your attitude plays an important role to have a success. Keep yourself and your attitude very positive to be in the line of successful people, because life never waits for you, if you are not capable to do it, someone else will do it, so when we know we can't do but someone else can do means it can also be done by me, just the problem is that we are on the wrong track, we just have to correct our track and move on.

Now when we move ahead in our life of success, we still have to concentrate on the path, because the path which is smooth right now can also be rough ahead, so we have to take proper care of our each and every steps that we take. Even don't hesitate to step back if you find that the path is going to end without destination, because you might have taken wrong path and we need to go back to choose the correct one.

"Define your Success with your work, not with what you get or not"- Jaymin Shah

Anushka

Anushka is a young writer and a poet who relishes delineating the nature's charm and positiveness in words with alacrity. She writes quotes, one-liners, and microtales. According to her 'Poetry is like a sword, which can even slash the oceans of negativity and despair and create a path of optimism and faith.'

Rape: A Nasty Loophole

Ya I stand for myself,
So, why there is no one by my side!?
Why always they support "men",
And why my rights are denied...!?

These demons, these nasty ones;
Why there atrocious thoughts are fulfilled!?
Why people slay a girl, and cradle these kinda "sons"!?
 Just for satisfying their salacity, every minute a girl is killed!?

For what they have an ego!?
Why can't they understand the meaning of "NO"!?
How the hell, they are still breathing!?
And still this society says, "It was just one rape case, let it go"

These animals don't have any right to live.
So why their coffin are still empty!?
Why do I suffer for there natsy deeds!?
Actually my success is the reason of their envy!

They should be hung; executed; shot off at the gun point,
So that they would aquaint to hell...
And these "men" should get it right in their mind,
That a girl is not there to be their victim...
If she can be silent, she can also rebel...!

(2)

Sometimes it feels empty....
Sometimes the feelings twine....
Sometimes it feels bitty....
But all we say is;"It's fine!"

(3)

Your suffering has a purpose;
It will end soon, just be patient!
And life without sufferings is like an adventure without
storms...

(4)

A star said to the moon...
Maybe I look small but I have my own light!
And this goes on in our lives!

Monica Prajapati

Monica Prajapati an energetic 19 year girl born in Gujarat. With a positive attitude to learn something new, she was fascinated with the music in her life, and this interest led to some early exposure to sing or play musical instruments, with that she had a very great interest in reading, since she was drawn to stories related to Music and Motivations Later, Ms. Monica, who is now a **socialist** and a **law graduate**, created a passion for ideas. The below written lines can very well define her.

I saw Girl with a cute smile,
She thinks with a beautiful mind.
She bothers, she worries, she cries,
For the one she says you are mine.
I saw Girl with a cute smile
        ~ Jaymin Shah.

The Way I Think.

"Something which makes You Clear, with what's not familiar in two or more things is nothing but a difference" ~ **Monica Prajapati.**

Talking about a thing which is predictive bit in the actual scenario it's far different from our predictions. We don't know what life has kept for us but according to my belief everything happens for a reason. It always tells us or teaches us a new chapter in life.

What do we live for?? When our ultimate goal is death. Life gives us chances to achieve the goal in different ways and every single thing or being achieves it. We make predictions for what will happen but in real sense it depends on what we are doing today. It's just the outcome that we did today. It's the imaginary box where we store out imaginations, dreams, goals, plans and so on. Imagining things, making plans, overthinking on what will happen in the next moment is just ruining our present.

Yes we can make plans, think, imagine but it should be in a positive way, the negative way is only destroying what we are having in the present. No one knows what has kept in that mystery box so why worrying about it if it's good that's great and if it's bad it's great too. The reason is it will teach something directly or indirectly to us. If you can't do anything about it, don't worry about it. The only thing we can do is just imagine it or predict it because we can't change what will be happening tomorrow. What's coming is better than what is gone and will get better may be we like it or not.

We just get a chance daily to make our "sabra ka fal more sweet". We want it to be sweet but it will be a mixture of the flavors spicy, bitter, sour, and sweet. We don't know what will happen but we know one thing that if we lose people/things thinking they will not be with us in future it's ultimately ruining the present when we have them. It will be decided you deserve that thing or not in future but meanwhile if you have it grab it don't lose it by thinking it will be taken away.

"Want to say something, tell it;
Want to do something, do it;
Why to wait when you know;
it might be an end."

Devamrutha S

In her own bubble, yet trying to merge with many more. A 22 year old student who just rediscovered her love for writing once again while she revisited some of her old musings.
Still trying to figure out how carpe diem really works, and taking life one day at a time.
Even though people say there's nothing in a name, she believes her name very much reflects her personality. Invinsible ideas and immortal will power, nothing more than her name, could describe her better.

Reality Resurrection

Baffled I sat, point blank, giving up on life, and on self.
Clutched with loneliness and stabbed with pain,
I lived in my dreams, which was my only solace.

Not the cliched ones I saw here, every place so alive and near.
Where dreams and reality juxtaposed, my life, thus began.

My eyes went seeking for someone, beyond bare spaces.
This Stranger I remember marked the inception of joy.

I rifled the glance of that face, an ecstasy it induced in me.
The throbbing heart of mine craved, to vanquish all pain that ever remained.

Merged in his talk, my heart skipped a beat,
Or maybe even two.
His eyes had the shine of a thousand stars, bringing me back to life, and again.

Time flew by, waiting for none.
The Sun, the same, but we are old.
Everyday shorter of breath, yet everyday high on life.

And now when I see that face, that has always been my haven.
A voice within me whispers, 'He'll always be a stranger you knew, since Adam was a lad'.

If At All...

If at all,
A chance was a treasure,
that you never wanted to give.
Take away these memories too,
till now which I have treasured.

I lay my vision on those days,
where happiness I could feel in the air.
How I long to get those back,
but neither of the hopes survived.

Actions turn out to be void,
words, they never existed,
But memories crawled in.
Why not take those back,
which I never wanted to give?

Protect your heart people,
striving no more wins.
This triumph can't be had,
maybe it was never mine.

This defeat is never a lesson,
Trapped in between love and sheer loneliness.
Sure did you win, but I never lost.

Sourav Malakar

I am sourav malakar from West Bengal. I am a **motivational speaker, writer, artist** and **a social media influencer.**
Follow me on instagram: **@sourav._.malakar**

Trapted Addiction

Usdin jab hum ghar aye tab ek dost ka massage aya hua tha to maine check kia.

wo mera school mate tha, to maine uska massage padha and i am shocked usme likha hua tha ki "gourav" ne suicide kar lia ! Mujhe aab janna tha ki gourav ne suicide kue kia to maine mere dost ko call kia jisne massage kia tha, but uska phone switch off tha. Fir maine gourav ke our ke dost ko call kia to usne call receive kia.

Humne pucha bro gourav ke bare mai kuch suna kya?

Fir dost ne puri kahani mujhe khulkar bataai.

End me mujhe ye pata chala ki "gourav" depression me tha because use koi pasand nahi karta tha, just because wo nasha ke addiction me trap ho gaya tha. Nashe ke waze se uska body structure bhi bigar gaya tha, Aakhe andar ghusi hui maano koi jinda lash jaisa. Nasha na chor pana uske life me bar bar problem create kar raha tha. As a result he is no more. Kisi dusre ke sath aisa naho iska solution kya hai?

"7777 technique" ek aisa technique hai jiske madat se koi bhi kisibhi tarha ka nasha chor sakta hai. Ye technique bohut logoko nashe ki dunia se bahar laya hai.

1 aadmi tha jo dinbhar me ₹ 500 kamate tha baki time drugs leta tha to income badhti nahi thi,

Unka ek family tha jo unper dependent tha.

Family me maa, biwi, uski beti thi, uski beti class 9 me thi to padhai likhai ka kharcha chalane ke lie unki biwi ko bhi job per jana padta tha.Jo bhi ho, bohut mushkil se unka gujara ho jata tha.

Kue ki wo aad mi 7 saal se drugs ke addiction me tha to unka income me se kuch bhi wo gharme nahi de pata tha.

Ekdin wo aadmi bolraha tha mai 7 saal se drugs pita hu, chorna chata hu but chor nahi pa raha.

Unhone bola: - bohut kuch kia lekin chor nahi paya...

Fir humne unhe "7777 technique" ke bareme bola... Or ghar chala aya

14 -15 din baad unse raste me hamari firse mulakat hui,

Unhone bola: - abhi bina drugs kebhi rahsakta hu .aab gharme bhi sab thik thak hai. Bus kabhi kabhi drugs le leta hu, koi dost samne laye to.

(Fir 5-6 din baad jab unse mila)

Unhone bola: - bhai chalo mere sath.

Humne bola: - kaha?

Fir unhone mereliye chocolate kharida or mujhe dia or unke ghar lunch ka amantran bhi dia...

Or unhone bola: humne drugs chor dia...

Or mai abhi dinka ₹ 1000 kamata hu agle mahine se ₹ 25000 ghar pe de paunga.

To inki life to thik ho gaya, Ab wo aadmi bohut khush bhi hai.

To "7777 technique" asal mai hai kya?

Iska sadharan sa jawab hai

(7days × 4weeks = 28days)

28 days agar aapne jit lia to puri life aapko kisibhi nasha ke age harna nahi hoga.

•To 28 days hame kya karna hoga?

•**Step 1**

hame ek chart banana hai

28 days ka, niche die hue chart ko follow karke aapna chart banate hai to ye best hoga.

1 2 3 4 5 6 7 (1st week) - 50% day

1 2 3 4 5 6 7 (2nd week) - 25% day

1 2 3 4 5 6 7 (5th week) - 15% for 4 days

1 2 3 4 5 6 7 (4th week) - no addiction

•**Step2**

Aapne pure din ka nasha ka quantity pata kijie.

or uska 50% nasha aap pahle 7 din (1st week) me kijie.

•Step3

(2nd week) me aap aapne nasha ki quantity 25% kam kar dijie.

•Step4

Abhi aapke pass bache hai last 7 days (4th week) abhi aap bus 15% nasha week ke 1,3,5,7 numbers din me kijie.

•Golden Step for Life

28 complete ho gaya hai aapne bohut nasha kar lia abhi is jindagi se bahar aa jaiye, dusro kobhi bahar aneme help kijie.

So aapne abhi tak jo bhi kia use bhulkar naye se suru kijie.

Nasha abhi aapke control me hai.

Abhi aap nashe ke control se bahar aachuke hai.

Congratulations....

Please help us to reach more people and make a happiest world.

WE CAN DO ANYTHING...

Thank you.

Aashtha Sisodiya

Aashtha Sisodiya is from Darbhanga, Bihar. She has completed her schooling in her hometown Darbhanga. She **loves to write poems and stories.** She follows her heart and wants to share her thoughts to people via poems and stories.
IG: @aashiyaapa

दोहरी समाज

रानी आज बहुत खुश है, अरे हो भी क्यों नहीं रानी और समीर दोनों एक ही दफ़्तर मे काम करते है और बेइंतहा प्यार भी। और आज इनदोनों कि शादी हो रही है।

रानी अपनी माँबाप की इकलौती संतान है और उसके पिताजी को गुज़रे २० वर्ष हो गए।

खैर रानी दुल्हन बनकर बहुत ही सुंदर लग रही है और समीर अपनी नजरे नहीं हटा पा रहा है , आज समीर को अपनी जिंदगी कि खवाहिश पूरी होती दिख रही है । रानी मंडप पर बैठी तभी अचानक से उसकी तबियत खराब हो गई , डॉक्टर को बुलाया गया , डॉक्टर ने बताया की रानी मां बनने वाली है, यह सुनते ही समीर और वहां खड़े लोगों के पैरों तले ज़मीन खिशक गई, लड़के वालों ने शादी तोड़ दी और लोगों ने बहुत खरी खोटी सुनाई ,सब कुछ बर्बाद होते देख रानी की मां कुषुम जी समीर की मां से बोली कि आप बेशक ही यह रिश्ता तोड़ दीजिए लेकीन इससे पहले कृपा कर मेरी बात सुन लीजिए।

बात २ महीने पहले की है रानी शाम सात बजे अपने दफ्तर से लौट रही थी तभी कुछ गुंडे ने उसके साथ जबदस्ती दुष्कर्म किया और यह बात मैने अपने मायके वालों को बताया क्योंकि घर में कोई मर्द नहीं होने कि वजह से मै बहुत डर गई थी, मेरे मायके वालो ने मुझे पुलिस में ना जाने की सलाह दी और बताया की पुलिस वाले बहुत गन्दी तरीके से पूछताछ करेंगे और समाज में लोग बाते भी बनाएंगे, वैसे भी घर में कोई मर्द नहीं होने के कारण लोग गन्दी नज़रों से देखते है लेकिन यह घटना के बाद तोह उनका जीना ही मुश्किल कर देंगे।

यह बात मुझे ठीक लगी और मैने चुप रहने में ही भलाई समझी, यह बोलते बोलते रानी कि मां रोने लग गई । यह सब सुन कर समीर ने रानी को इंसाफ दिलाने का वादा किया और उन दरिंदे को जेल

भिजवाया और खुशी खुशी रानी के साथ विवाह किया और दोनों अपने सपनो के घर को पूरा करने में लग गए।

यहीं इसी समाज मे कुछ लोग रेप पीड़िता के साथ दुर्व्यवहार करते है तो कुछ लोग इन्हें समझकर इन्हें इंसाफ दिलाकर इनकी मदद करते है, सच तो यह है कि समाज कि समझ हमसे बनती है ,हम जैसा सोचेंगे समाज कि सोच भी वैसी ही होगी, हम अगर रेप, अंतर्जातीय विवाह, विधवा विवाह को समझेंगे तो समाज भी समझेगा क्युकी हम समाज से नहीं बने है, समाज हमसे बना है।

यह दो मुखड़ा समाज है जहा परिवर्तन सब चाहते और समझते है, लेकिन जब वरिवर्तन करने कि बारी आती है तो समाज का नाम ले कर अपना कदम पिछे हटा लेते है।

परिवर्तन को समाज समझता तो है लेकिन कभी कभी बहुत देर हो जाती है, समाज के डर से ना जाने कितने लोगों को अपनी ईच्छा और सपने भूलने पड़ जाते है वहीं कुछ ग़लत कदम उठाते है।

जहा जरूरत परिवर्तन कि हो तो परिवर्तन करो और जहा जरूरत अपनी परंपरा कि है तो उसे भी दिल से निभाओ यहीं जीने का तरीका हमे सफल बनाएगी।

Flairs and Glairs, a platform by a student for the students. We are esteemed youth struggling to carve out our path for our future and we follow a basic mindset Since everyone is not born with all-round skills. Joining hands with people who are born to execute it with perfection is the best way to evolve. Self-Evolution is the need of the hour but, evolving as a community is what we strive for. The initiative as kickstarted by, Founder- Mr. Shubham Shah with the motive to utilize the skillset and talent of writing has now a team of 10+ people who are actively participating into newer forms of learning and discovering talents among youngsters. We Provide platform and services like Publishing opportunities, Open mics, Workshops, Hands-on training. Operating with Brand Name of Flairs and Glairs (Publication House), we offer the chance of elevating a passionate writer to an esteemed author With Brand name Teekhe Zasbaaat. We bring to you an opportunity to get accustomed with the Public Speaking and Presenting of Thoughts along with regular challenges to brush up your inking spirit. The newest initiative to extend our services we introduced in a new writing Platform- The Glittering Fables and Ink Over Tears.

We Choose to Fly Like A Falcon than to be

a Leg Pulling Crab.

To Know More: Infoline – 7781900870
Mail Us At-
flairsandglairs@gmail.com / info@flairsandglairs.in
Or Visit is at
www.flairsandglairs.com / www.flairsandglairs.in
Social Handles- @flairsandglairs @teekhezasbaaat